CHRISTMAS IN
NORTH CAROLINA

Sue Carabine

Illustrations by
Shauna Mooney Kawasaki

Gibbs Smith, Publisher

First Edition
07 06 05 04 03   5 4 3 2 1

Text and illustrations © 2003
by Gibbs Smith, Publisher

Published by
Gibbs Smith, Publisher
P.O. Box 667
Layton, Utah 84041

1-800-748-5439 orders
www.gibbs-smith.com

Edited by Linda Nimori
Designed and produced by Mary Ellen Thompson,
  TTA Design
Printed and bound in China

ISBN 1-58685-271-X

'Twas the night before Christmas,
all was ready to go:
St. Nick and his deer
had a full sleigh in tow,

When Nick slipped on ice
and then tried to grab hold
Of the brake, which popped back
and just knocked him out cold!

Mrs. Claus came out, running,
as quick as a wink,
To give poor aching Santa
a soothing hot drink.

"Sip slowly, my dear,"
she quite anxiously said.
"Are you able to travel?
Should I go instead?"

"I . . . I think I'll be fine,"
Santa said with a stammer,
"But my head feels as though
it's been hit with a hammer!

"What time is it? Day is it?
Is it November?
For the life of me, Mama,
I just can't remember!"

"My goodness, it's Christmas!
Oh, what shall we do?
We can't fill the stockings, dear,
not without you!"

Now, Dasher, quite worried
'cause Nick seemed subdued,
Told Dancer, "We must
get him right back on cue.

"You know how Nick always
heads first straight for China?
Well, this year let's fly
into North Carolina!

"It's Nick's favorite state,
where his memories are sweet.
Those great folks will help him
get back on his feet!

"Let's visit the Smokies
and fix up the sleigh
With handcrafted items—
it'll make Santa's day!

"Well, what do you think, guys?
Could this be a reality?
This state is well known for its
southern hospitality!"

All nodded, then flew off to
the great Tarheel State,
Where Nick would find pralines
and mud pies first rate!

Prancer scanned Santa's list
and knew right where to go.
There were special requests
to be dealt with below.

In no time, great looming
Mount Mitchell appeared,
Nick cried out, "That's awesome!"
as the summit drew near.

Along Blue Ridge Parkway,
o'er Land of Waterfalls,
Nick thought, "Seems familiar . . .
To me, this land calls."

In Asheville, folks gathered
in church, where they knelt
And softly gave thanks
in this staunch Bible Belt.

St. Nick said serenely,
"Folks here know the reason
We celebrate Christmas
and this holy season."

From Charlotte, they traveled
up mountain, through valley
Toward the capital named
after Sir Walter Raleigh.

As they flew o'er "The Rock"
(the great NASCAR speedway),
Nick spied a cool race car.
"I must try that! What say?"

He nosed the big sleigh
into one of the pits,
And quickly donned race gear,
then laughed, "Hey! It fits!"

Though his deer all declined,

they said, "Santa, you must!"

So he roared 'round the track

In a huge cloud of dust!

"I bet I'd win Winston
and Busch on this track,"
Nick mused as a guy waved
a bright checkered flag.

"It's the wrong time of year,"
called the guy with a grin,
"to race NASCAR drivers.
But, ya'll come again!"

Once more on their way,
Santa chanced to look down,
Saw something that caused him
to fly near the ground!

Elated, he cried,
"What a wonderful view!
We're o'er Winston-Salem,
Chapel Hill, Durham, too."

Then young Vixen giggled,
"I think Santa knows
Which basketball teams
are right under his nose!

"Please tell us now, Nick,
from your own point of view,
Will Duke beat Wake Forest
or NCSU?

"They've all got great teams
but quite soon some must drop;
Do you think UNC just might
come out on top?"

"No comment," Nick smiled
as he seemed to recall
How much this great state
loved their school basketball!

Then Comet cried out,
"Our course takes us due east
Through a storm that has caused
all the power to cease."

A letter from Patsy Ann
said, "Nick, take care.
If the weather is dreadful,
don't fret, you stay there!"

Nick chuckled, then mused,
"Ah, sweet Patsy, I'd walk
If I had to, to find you
in quaint Kitty Hawk."

"I believe that was one
of my most favorite flights,
Memory tells me I called on
some boys there named Wright."

Then, suddenly, they saw
an incredible sight:
The Outer Banks glowed with
soft shimmering light!

At a Yule-bedecked window,

Patsy Ann wore a grin.

"Oh, thank you, dear Santa.

You made it! Come in!"

Later on in their journey,
they saw while in flight
The spiral-shaped grid of
Cape Hatteras Light.

As Nick watched the beacon,
his eyes filled with tears
'Cause he felt this place held
long lost memories so dear.

Then Cupid drawled broadly,
"Now, y'all, nothin's finah
Than flyin' o'er famed
USS Nawth Care'lina!"

St. Nick cried, "You're right!
The folks here are so true
To their country, so proud
of the red, white, and blue!

"I see special gifts here
way down deep in my bag
For children of soldiers
at LeJeune and Fort Bragg.

"And, Wilmington's next!"
Donner passed Nick a letter,
And said, "It's from Michael,
who longs to feel better.

" 'Sometimes I am naughty,'
Mike wrote, 'sometimes nice.
I'd be good all the time
if I had some white mice.' "

On the roof, down the chimney,

Nick ne'er made a sound,

Tucked mice 'neath the tree,

paused to look all around.

He returned to the sleigh,
a strange look on his face.
"Didn't another lad live
fairly close to this place?

"He was also named Michael;
We left him a ball."
"That was Jordan," laughed Blitzen,
"he grew VERY tall!

"We also left boxing gloves
that very day
For a cute little Leonard boy
called Sugar Ray."

"Ho! Ho! Ho!" Santa boomed.
"My poor memory is back!
This mushy old brain, boys,
is now right on track!

"But, now, we must leave
these fine folks, this great state;
They've made us feel welcome.
Come, boys, we'll be late."

As snow softly powdered
the ski slopes in white,
Nick called, "Merry Christmas,
Carolinians, sleep tight!"